THIS CANDLEWICK BOOK BELONGS TO:

Amy Hest and Jill Barton have collaborated on all of the Baby Duck books. "When I saw Jill's illustrations for the first book," Amy recalls, "I loved them so much that I sat down and wrote two more stories about Baby Duck." There are now a total of seven books about this plucky duck heroine and her family. Amy Hest is the author of many other books for children, including the *New York Times* bestseller *Kiss Good Night*, illustrated by Anita Jeram, and middle-grade novels about another memorable heroine: *Love You, Soldier*; *The Private Notebooks of Katie Roberts, Age 11*; and *The Great Green Notebook of Katie Roberts*. The winner of three Christopher Medals, Amy Hest lives in New York City.

Jill Barton drew on her memories of her own grandfather to illustrate the Baby Duck books. "He always made the time to listen," she recalls. Jill Barton is the illustrator of many picture books, including *The Caterpillow Fight* by Sam McBratney, *It's Quacking Time!* by Martin Waddell, and *Lady Lollipop* and *Clever Lollipop* by Dick King-Smith.

Then Baby Duck hopped and skipped into the big schoolhouse with her new friend Davy Duck.

She sang a pretty song.

"Off to school, Baby Duck!
I am big and brave.
I like Miss Posy, Davy Duck too.
And I'll have fun in school!"

But Hot Stuff cried,
"Wa, waa,
waaaa!"

Baby Duck put her arm
around Hot Stuff.
"Little small babies have
to wait," she said.

She gave Hot Stuff
the picture she had
made. "Chin up!"
Baby said.

Miss Posy rang the bell.
"Good luck," Grampa said,
shaking Baby's hand.

Then Mr. and Mrs. Duck
took turns kissing
Baby on both
cheeks.

"We'll be right here,"
they promised,
"when school
lets out."

"Do you read books in there?" Grampa asked.

"Oh, yes!" said Miss Posy.

"Do you like sandwiches with jam, and yellow pencils?" Grampa asked.

"Oh, yes!" said Miss Posy.

Miss Posy came across the schoolyard.

"My name is Miss Posy," she said.

"I'm the teacher."

"Are you mean?" Grampa asked.

"Oh, no!" said Miss Posy.

"Do you sing songs in that
schoolhouse?" Grampa asked.

"Oh, yes!" said Miss Posy.

Then Baby drew a picture.

Davy Duck took little steps toward Baby.

He looked at Baby's picture.

Baby felt proud.

After that Baby showed Grampa
the important things inside her school bag.
He liked the pencil from Hot Stuff.
"You draw nice pictures, Baby,"
Grampa pointed out.
"Yes," Baby said. "I do."

"I will," Grampa said.
And he buckled Baby's shoe.

"Sometimes it helps to sing a song,"
Grampa said. "You sing nice songs, Baby."
"Yes," Baby said. "I do." Then Baby sang a song.

"Please don't make me go to school.
My teacher will be mean.
I won't have any fun or friends.
And who will buckle my new shoe?"

"Calling all babies! Here I am!"
Grampa was waiting on a bench.
Baby sat right up close to Grampa.
"Rough day?" he whispered.
"Yes," Baby said.
"Long walk?" whispered Grampa.
"Yes," Baby said.
"Scared about school?"
whispered Grampa.
"Yes," Baby said.
"Yes, yes, yes!"

The Duck family waddled down the road. "Hop to it, Baby!" called Mr. Duck.
Baby could not hop. Her feet felt too heavy.

"Chin up, Baby!" called Mrs. Duck. "Skip along!" Baby could not skip. Her school bag was bumping. *Bumpity bumpity bump.*

The Duck family waddled to the big school-house. Baby's buckle popped open and now her shoe was flapping. *Flappity flappity flap.*

Mr. and Mrs. Duck bustled out the front
door, swinging Hot Stuff in the air.
Their feet crunched on dry leaves.
"Come, come!" they cried.
"School, glorious school!"
Baby Duck dragged behind.
"Goodbye, house," she whispered
in a little small voice.

Mr. Duck looked at his watch.
"Time to go!" he cried.

"Button up your new
school sweater!"
called Mrs. Duck.
"Hurry, Baby!"

Baby buttoned. It took a long time.

"Buckle up your new
school shoes!"
called Mr. Duck.
"Hurry, Baby!"

Baby buckled. It took a long time.

Baby Duck sat under the table
with her blue school bag.
Baby loved her school bag,
and the important things inside:
one favorite book,
a sandwich with jam,
one tall pad,
and one yellow pencil
(a special going-to-school
present from
Hot Stuff).

"Your sister Hot Stuff is way too small
   to go to school," Mrs. Duck pointed out.
"She's not brave enough, either.
   Aren't you glad to be big and brave?"
"No," Baby said.

Baby Duck could not eat her breakfast.
It was the first day of school,
and her stomach was all jitters!
"Breakfast toast is very tasty," said Mrs. Duck.
"Won't you have a bite?"
"No," Baby said.
"Breakfast juice is very juicy," said Mr. Duck.
"Won't you have a sip?"
"No," Baby said.

Off to School, Baby Duck!

Amy Hest

illustrated by **Jill Barton**

CANDLEWICK PRESS
CAMBRIDGE, MASSACHUSETTS

For Hannah and Zoe,

a couple of first-rate schoolgirls

A. H.

For Alex and Bump

J. B.

Text copyright © 1999 by Amy Hest
Illustrations copyright © 1999 by Jill Barton

First U.S. paperback edition 2001

The Library of Congress has cataloged the hardcover edition as follows:

Hest, Amy.
Off to school, Baby Duck! / Amy Hest ; illustrated by Jill Barton. — 1st ed.
p. cm.
Summary: Baby Duck experiences the fear of the first day of school, but
with a little help from Grampa, everything turns out okay in the end.
ISBN 978-0-7636-0244-4 (hardcover)
[1. First day of school—Fiction. 2. Fear—Fiction. 3. Grandfathers—Fiction.
4. Ducks—Fiction.] I. Barton, Jill, ill. II. Title.
PZ7.H43750f 1999
[E]—dc21   98-51312

ISBN 978-0-7636-3438-4 (paperback)

Previously published in paperback with the ISBN 978-0-7636-1054-8

2 4 6 8 10 9 7 5 3

Printed in China

This book was typeset in Opti Lucius Ad Bold.
The illustrations were done in pencil and watercolor.

Candlewick Press
2067 Massachusetts Avenue
Cambridge, Massachusetts 02140

visit us at www.candlewick.com